MARTIN LUTHER KING JR. DAY

HOLIDAYS

Lynda Sorensen

The Rourke Press, Inc.
Vero Beach, Florida 32964

Edited by Sandra A. Robinson

PHOTO CREDITS
All photos © Flip Schulke

Library of Congress Cataloging-in-Publication Data

Sorensen, Lynda, 1953-
    Martin Luther King, Jr., day / Lynda Sorensen.
    p. cm. — (Holidays)
    ISBN 1-57103-068-9
    1. Martin Luther King, Jr., Day—Juvenile literature.
2. King, Martin Luther, Jr., 1929-1968—Juvenile literature.
I. Title. II. Series: Sorensen, Lynda, 1953- Holidays.
E185.97.K5S64   1994
323'.092—dc20   94-17840
                                                          CIP
Printed in the USA   AC

TABLE OF CONTENTS

MARTIN LUTHER KING JR. DAY

Martin Luther King Jr. Day celebrates the life and ideas of Dr. Martin Luther King Jr., a famous African American. This **national** American holiday is celebrated on the third Monday in January.

Dr. King's courage and ideas helped black Americans gain more power and freedom in their country.

Dr. King worked and lived in places where many white Americans were angry at him. He was cursed, spit at, arrested and jailed. Even so, Dr. King worked throughout his life in the ways of peace, not anger.

Dr. Martin Luther King Jr. was arrested and jailed for protesting against segregation in America

THE EARLY YEARS

Martin Luther King Jr. was born on January 15, 1929, in Atlanta, Georgia. He was the son of a Baptist minister. The church was an important part of young Martin's life.

Dr. King graduated from Morehouse College in 1948. Afterward he studied at Crozer Seminary in Chester, Pennsylvania, to become a minister.

At Crozer, Dr. King learned about Mohandas Gandhi. Gandhi had been an important leader of his people in India.

Dr. King began his career as a minister

A STUDENT OF GANDHI

Gandhi wanted the British rulers of India to leave his country. He asked the Indian people to peacefully disobey laws that were unfair to them. Gandhi's protests were entirely **nonviolent.** Neither he nor his followers used guns, knives or fists.

Martin Luther King Jr. was impressed by Gandhi's life. He later chose Gandhi's nonviolent methods to deal with problems faced by African Americans.

Dr. King led peaceful marches of protest, but marchers often needed police protection against mobs

SEGREGATION

In the early 1950s, one of the biggest problems for African Americans was **segregation.** This was the practice of keeping white and black Americans apart.

In some places in the North and the South, segregation was a custom, a practice 300 years old. It was also law in some parts of the South.

Black people could not share public schools with white students in the South. Many hotels, restaurants and other public buildings were either "White Only" or they had separate "black" and "white" areas.

Dr. King, his wife Coretta and their followers marched to protest segregation

At the Lincoln Memorial in Washington, D.C., Dr. King spoke of "the dream"
he had for his children and his country

Dr. King's civil rights movement gave hope of new tomorrows for thousands of black Americans

THE BUS BOYCOTT

Unfair laws were part of life for African Americans in the South. In Montgomery, Alabama, black bus riders had to give up their seats if white riders couldn't find a seat.

Martin Luther King Jr. was a pastor in Montgomery in 1955. He asked black people to **boycott,** or quit using, the buses. They agreed.

The Montgomery bus system finally stopped segregation. More importantly, the U.S. Supreme Court in 1956 ruled that segregation on buses was illegal.

Dr. King met with President John F. Kennedy (right) and other national leaders to find peaceful solutions to problems

THE SOUTHERN CHRISTIAN LEADERSHIP CONFERENCE

Dr. King's work in Montgomery was noticed by many other people. He was elected president of a group of black ministers called the Southern Christian Leadership Conference (SCLC).

The SCLC organized marches, protests and **sit-ins** to change unfair practices toward black people. During sit-ins, black people moved into "White Only" restaurants and sat down. Instead of being served, they were usually arrested. Eventually, though, the SCLC's nonviolent protests were rewarded by progress in civil rights.

Andrew Young (left), Dr. King (center) and other black leaders worked through the SCLC and other black organizations

CIVIL RIGHTS

Much of Dr. King's work dealt with *civil rights,* the basic rights and freedoms of citizens. Dr. King simply wanted equal and fair treatment for African Americans. Black people weren't getting fair treatment in areas such as schooling, housing, voting rights and public transportation.

Dr. King's work helped lead to the Civil Rights Bill of 1964. This national law made any segregation illegal. It also gave black people equal opportunities under the laws of the United States.

Dr. King spoke out for the civil rights
of all Americans

"I HAVE A DREAM ..."

On August 28, 1963, Dr. King spoke to a crowd of over 200,000 black and white Americans. The crowd had gathered at the Lincoln Memorial in Washington, D.C., to protest laws that were unfair to black Americans.

"I have a dream," Dr. King said that day, "that my four little children will one day live in a nation where they will not be judged by the color of their skin, but by the content of their character."

Dr. King's stirring words that day later became known as his "I Have a Dream" speech.

Dr. King spoke to a crowd of more than 200,000 Americans at the Lincoln Memorial in 1963

HONORING DR. MARTIN LUTHER KING JR.

During his brief lifetime, Dr. King won a Nobel Prize for Peace. He was *Time* magazine's Man of the Year in 1962.

Dr. King was murdered on April 4, 1968, in Memphis, Tennessee. After her husband's death, Mrs. Coretta Scott King formed the Martin Luther King Jr. Center for Nonviolent Social Change in America.

In 1980 the National Park Service established a Martin Luther King Jr. National Historic Site.

Dr. King was also honored with the national holiday bearing his name.

Glossary

boycott (BOY kaht) — to refuse to buy, sell or use something, usually to force a change in a situation

national (NAH shun ul) — of or relating to a nation

nonviolent (non VI uh lent) — done without force or bloodshed

segregation (sehg re GAY shun) — keeping groups of people separate and apart on purpose

sit-in (SIT in) — taking seats in a segregated place to protest segregation

INDEX